The Sleepover Club

Have you been invited to all these sleepovers?

Sleepover Girls Go Splash!

by Sue Mongredien

Collins

An imprint of HarperCollins*Publishers*

The Sleepover Club ® is a
registered trademark of HarperCollins*Publishers* Ltd

First published in Great Britain by Collins in 2001
Collins is an imprint of HarperCollins*Publishers* Ltd
77-85 Fulham Palace Road, Hammersmith,
London, W6 8JB

The HarperCollins website address is
www.fireandwater.com

3 5 7 9 8 6 4 2

Text copyright © Sue Mongredien 2001
Title by Jess Mannion
Strapline by Lily Appiah

Original series characters, plotlines
and settings © Rose Impey 1997

ISBN 0 00710539 8

The author asserts the moral right to
be identified as the author of the work.

Printed and bound in Great Britain by
Omnia Books Limited, Glasgow

Sleepover Kit List

1. Sleeping bag
2. Pillow
3. Pyjamas or a nightdress
4. Slippers
5. Toothbrush, toothpaste, soap etc
6. Towel
7. Teddy
8. A creepy story
9. Food for a midnight feast:
   chocolate, crisps, sweets, biscuits.
   In fact anything you like to eat.
10. Torch
11. Hairbrush
12. Hair things like a bobble or hairband,
    if you need them
13. Clean knickers and socks
14. Change of clothes for the next day
15. Sleepover diary and membership card

CHAPTER ONE

Hello! It's Lyndz here. How's it going? It's ages and ages since I've seen you – sorry! Don't think I've been neglecting you, but I'm just always soooo busy – I've been down at the stables helping out every chance I get, you see. Just for you, though, I'm going to make a real effort and tell you all about the time the Sleepover Club made a great big SPLASH!

I can remember the exact moment it all started. It was a Thursday morning and a horrible rainy February day. Ugh! February is just THE worst month, don't you think? It's so grey and gloomy – and all the nice things like summer and my birthday and Christmas seem ages and ages away. I was shivering in the playground before school that morning, wishing Spring would hurry up and come soon, so we might actually get a bit of sunshine again.

Also, to make it even worse, Mrs Weaver, our class teacher, had declared it 'mental arithmetic week' and was giving us these gruesome maths tests every single morning. Honestly! How mean can you get? I'm not very good at Maths – in fact, I'm rubbish – so I wasn't looking forward to going into lessons at all.

Anyway, I soon cheered up when Kenny bounded into the playground, with a grin stretching from ear to ear. When she's in one of her bouncy moods, she reminds me of our dog, Buster. He's a little Jack Russell, and has more energy than any creature I've ever known. You can't feel miserable with Buster around – it's impossible!

"Guess what?" Kenny said excitedly, once she'd spotted us and run over.

"They've discovered life on Mars?" Frankie said hopefully.

"School has been cancelled today?" I suggested, thinking about the maths test.

"Something about football probably," Fliss said, not looking terribly interested.

"You've cracked the meaning of life?" was Rosie's guess.

Kenny beamed. "Oh, none of those," she said airily. "This is MUCH better! I was at swimming club last night and guess what?"

"Do we really have to guess again?" groaned Fliss.

"We don't know! Tell us, for goodness' sake!" Rosie said, laughing.

"Well, there's going to be a sponsored swim at Cuddington Baths in a couple of weeks, and I thought it would be a brilliant thing for the Sleepover Club to do," Kenny said breathlessly. "And there's going to be a big party afterwards and everything! So what do you all think?"

There was a pause while we took this in. Then...

Ooh! Hang on! I just thought. Have you met

all of us in the Sleepover Club? How rude of me not to even ask, eh? Hopefully you'll know everyone, but if you don't – or if you've just plain forgotten – I'd better dish the details before I go any further, or you won't have a clue what I'm on about.

Well! As I said, Kenny's a bit like my bouncy Buster – she's full of beans, full of fun, and full of get-up-and-go. She's a total Sporty Spice, too – when she's not swimming, she's playing football in the park with all the boys, or doing back flips at gymnastics club, or netball training, or... She's amazing! She's one of those people who are just naturally brilliant at every sport they do.

She's also an ace mate because she's dead loyal, and would do anything for you. If anyone ever tries to pick on one of us, Kenny's straight in there, backing us up with a fierce glint in her eye. And believe me, no-one in our class has the bottle to muck about with Kenny. She could out-fight everyone – even all the boys, I reckon!

Then there's Frankie. Wherever Kenny is, Frankie's usually with her, as the two of them are best friends. The only things they don't do together are all Kenny's sports stuff. It's not like Frankie's no good at sports, because she is, but she'd rather spend her spare time designing her very own rocket launch or painting her bedroom silver! Frankie's a bit eccentric, if you hadn't gathered. Sometimes I listen to her telling us about one of her brilliant ideas, and I just wonder what on earth she's on about this time. She's the cleverest one of us five by miles.

What else can I tell you about Frankie? Well, if Kenny's a bit like a bouncy Jack Russell, I'd compare Frankie to a chameleon or maybe even one of those fabulously coloured butterflies! Something funky and exotic, anyway, as Frankie wears the brightest, most outrageous things you've ever seen. She especially loves silver, which is her all-time favourite colour, but she's had a big purple phase lately. She even wanted to dye her hair purple, but her mum went mad at the thought and put her foot down in a big way. So sparkly purple nail varnish is about her limit right now.

I think Frankie always looks cool in a weird kind of style, but Fliss would disagree with that, I'm sure. Fliss – short for Felicity – is fashion queen of the Sleepover Club, although that's not difficult, to be honest. What with Kenny permanently in footy top and tracky bottoms, me in my scruffy jodhpurs, Frankie in one of her wild and wonderful outfits and Rosie in her sister's hand-me-downs, Fliss doesn't exactly have a lot of competition, clothes-wise.

I think Fliss gets her girly side from her mum, who's also mega into having perfectly groomed hair, manicured hands, and immaculate clothes. Fliss's idea of heaven is being able to spend thousands of pounds on clothes and beauty stuff. Her bedroom is amazing. As well as blinding you with its pinkness and girlyness, it's like being in a clothes shop, complete with matching accessories for EVERYTHING!

If you ask me, Fliss is a bit like a peacock – especially the boy peacocks who have those beautiful tails and are always showing them off. Sometimes, before she even says

"Hello", Fliss is asking you if you like her new top and telling you how much it cost. Definitely peacock behaviour!

Now, the big news about Fliss is that she's just become a big sister all over again – this time to two tiny baby twins!! Her mum had them a couple of weeks ago and they're just soooo cute. One boy and one girl, called Joseph (Joe for short) and Hannah, with identical snub noses and bald heads. Oh yeah, and not forgetting the identical screams!

I think Fliss was secretly hoping for two girls as she's not mad keen on little brothers (she's already got one – Callum). But she's dead chuffed with the twins, and loves helping her mum dress them up in all their cute little outfits. All together now… AHHH!

So as well as being a peacock, our Fliss has also become something of a mother hen these days. Although she does get cross when they cry all the way through *Neighbours* so she can't hear what anyone's saying.

And last but not least there's Rosie. Now, if Rosie were an animal or bird, I think she'd be a crab. First of all, because that's her birth sign, Cancerian, but also because she can be quite crabby at times. Most of the time she's great fun and really makes me laugh, but, just like a crab, she's got this very sensitive side under her hard shell. And boy, can she get in a mood at times!

Mind you, she has her reasons, I suppose. I won't make a big deal out of it, because she hates that, but Rosie's family are pretty hard up most of the time. Her dad left them a year or so ago and her mum really struggles with money. Tiffany, Rosie's big sister, has got a Saturday job so she's helping out a bit now, but there's still not really enough cash to go round.

Also, even though Rosie would never say so, I think she feels a bit left out at home sometimes. Her brother, Adam, has cerebral palsy and is in a wheelchair, and so their mum gives him a lot more attention than she does to Rosie. It would probably be different if her dad was still around, but when there's just one parent and three kids to look after, someone's bound to miss out on the attention somewhere, don't you think?

And last but not least there's me – Lyndsey Marianne Collins, although everyone just calls me Lyndz. Much easier, don't you think? I've got two big brothers and two little brothers and NO sisters – aaargh! Yes, it's wall-to-wall boys in our house, apart from me and Mum. You might think that's a nightmare if you hate boys, but it's actually OK. My favourite is my little baby brother Sam. Everyone calls him Spike because he has this great big tuft of hair sticking up at the front. He's soooo sweet and cuddly!

Now, if you know anything about me, you'll know that I absolutely love animals with a mad, mad passion. Sometimes I think I get on better with animals than people! I go horse riding every weekend, which is just my favourite thing in the world. My brother Stuart works part-time at a farm down the road from us, and I sometimes help muck out the horses there. Horses are just gorgeous, don't you think? They're so beautiful and strong and clever.

My favourite horse at the riding school is called Alfie. He's a gorgeous bay gelding with a white star in the middle of his forehead. I always take him some sugar lumps for a treat because they're his absolute favourite. Whenever he sees me, he nuzzles at my pockets with a hopeful whinny!

As well as Buster the dog, we've got three cats at home – Toffee, Truffle and Fudge. Truffle is my top cat because she's lovely and snuggly and sometimes sleeps in my bed with me. The three of them pick on Buster though, if they catch him eating their cat food. They all gang up on him and chase him round the garden together. It's one of the funniest things I've ever seen!

So what animal am I like, then? Well, the others gave me the nickname of Squirrel for a while, as Frankie reckoned I always had some sweets squirrelled away in my desk or in my bag. But I think that makes me sound more like a PIG!

If I could *choose* what animal I was, I'd be a horse, as I think they're just the best animals in the world. In fact, I think I'd choose to be Alfie, as he's so completely beautiful. Anyway, as I'm the one telling you all this, I think it's only fair that I should be allowed to pick what I'd be.

There you are then, that's us five. The Sleepover Club, yay! It's great being in a club with your four best mates. We try and have a sleepover every Friday night unless someone's on holiday or poorly, and we always do loads of cool stuff together at the weekends and in the school holidays. Best of all, someone's always coming up with an awesome idea of what the club can do next.

And that was where I'd got up to, wasn't it? Kenny's awesome idea. Let me start another chapter and I'll tell you more about it!

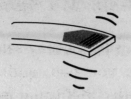

CHAPTER TWO

If you can remember that far back, before I so rudely interrupted the story, Kenny had just suggested that we all went in for this sponsored swim at Cuddington Baths.

"I'm going to go for my personal best – one hundred lengths!" she said, eyes gleaming with excitement. Kenny's a brilliant swimmer, of course. She's got her gold lifesavers' medal already, which is pretty spectacular for someone her age, apparently.

"A hundred lengths?" echoed Fliss, looking a bit faint at the thought. "We don't all have to swim that far, do we?"

"No, of course not, silly," Kenny said. "You just do as much as you can, and people sponsor you per length. Or, if you don't think you're going to manage many lengths, you can get them to give you a lump sum, like two pounds or something, just for taking part."

"I could probably only do about ten lengths – if that!" I said doubtfully. "I mean, I like the idea, but I can still only do doggy paddle. I haven't really got the hang of any other strokes yet."

"Ten lengths would be excellent!" Kenny said warmly. "We can all practise together at weekends. And I could teach you breaststroke if you want – it's dead easy. If you can do doggy paddle, you can easily do that."

"All right, thanks!" I said.

"I reckon I can do fifteen lengths – or maybe even twenty," Fliss said thoughtfully. She had a load of private swimming lessons last summer and is quite good now – even if she does hate getting her hair wet!

"I'm going to go for half a mile – thirty-two lengths," Frankie said excitedly. She goes swimming quite a lot with her dad, and often with Kenny, too, so she's pretty fit. "Half a mile – it sounds a long way, doesn't it?"

"Oh, you can do that, no problem," Kenny said confidently. "How about you, Rosie?"

"Ooh yes, of course, because you're a water sign, aren't you, Rosie?" Fliss said at once. We called her 'mystic Flisstic' for a while last summer, because she got really into horoscopes and fortune-telling. "You should be the best swimmer of the lot, then!"

Rosie went a bit pink. "I don't think so!" she said. She was trying to laugh but she looked a bit awkward about it. "Anyway, I don't think I'll be able to do the swimathon with you guys. Sorry, but..."

"But what?" Frankie said. "One for all, and all for one, remember, Rosie?"

Rosie bit her lip. She was looking dead shifty, which is unusual when she's normally such a down-to-earth person. "Well, the fact that my cozzie is so ancient and small that it's practically unwearable for starters," she said, with this embarrassed sort of laugh. "I don't think Cuddington is ready to see my bare bum hanging out!"

"Oh, I've got loads of swimming costumes," Fliss said at once. "You can borrow one of mine! Not my new one, obviously, as I'll be wearing that, but I'll dig out another one for you, if you like!"

"Nice one, Fliss!" I said. Fliss isn't often very generous with her things. She'd never lend me or Kenny any of her clothes, I'm sure, simply because she would worry that we'd rip them or stretch them! Mind you, I suppose a swimming costume is pretty hard to break, isn't it?

"Thanks, Fliss," Rosie said, but she still wasn't looking anyone in the eye. "But—"

"Anyway, you've GOT to take part," Kenny said suddenly. "Because I haven't told you the rest of it yet. All the money that we raise goes to Whizz-Kidz, I forgot to say! NOW tell me you won't take part!"

"Whizz-Kidz?" asked Frankie. "Who are they?"

"Oh!" Rosie said. She looked delighted at the news. "Whizz-Kidz is that charity for disabled kids. They make all these amazing customised wheelchairs and trikes and stuff.

You know that day centre that Adam goes to? They helped them out with a load of new wheelchairs, remember me telling you?"

"Yeah, and that's not all," Kenny said. "I can't believe I forgot to tell you all about this! After the swimathon, there's going to be this mega party at the pool for all the swimmers who take part, plus all their families. It should be really fab!"

Fliss's eyes lit up. "Ooh, I hope the lifeguards are good-looking!"

"Yeah, one of them's gorgeous, actually," Kenny said, winking at the rest of us. "Nige, he's called. I reckon you'll like him, Fliss."

"Oh, really?" Fliss said, smoothing her hair down. "What's he like, then?"

"Well..." said Kenny, but just then Mrs Poole blew the whistle and we had to go inside for registration. But from the wink Kenny had just given, I had a fair idea that 'Nige' wasn't going to be quite as hunky as Fliss was hoping!

Not even the morning maths test could dampen our spirits now we had the swimathon to get us excited! I couldn't stop thinking about it, and I could tell the others felt the same.

The only person who still didn't seem that interested was Rosie. But I guessed it was because she didn't have a swimming costume and felt embarrassed about it. Rosie's dead proud like that. When we first started hanging out with her, she wouldn't let us come round to her house for ages because she thought we'd turn our noses up at it, just because it's in a bit of a state!

To be honest, I think our house is much scruffier than hers, because my dad's one of these people who's always starting things off and never finishing them. So we've got a half-built wall here, a half-painted room there, a frame out the back for a conservatory that he's never managed to finish... It drives you mad sometimes!

Anyway, I don't mind the others seeing our mad half-built house because that's the way it's always been, but I guess Rosie's a bit different. I knew she'd hate having to wear one of Fliss's swimming costumes because she hates not being able to "pay her own way", as she says. But if something's offered to you, you might as well take it, in my book.

I was just imagining myself doing the most graceful breaststroke ever up and down Cuddington Baths with crowds of people cheering me on, when Mrs Weaver called out, "OK, time's up! Pens down!" and I realised with a jump that I'd barely started on the maths test. Uh-oh – I'd been day-dreaming again.

"OK, swap tests with the person next to you," Mrs Weaver said briskly. "Here are the answers. One – three nines are twenty-seven. Two – eighteen plus sixteen is thirty-four. Three – six fours are twenty-four..."

Luckily, I had Kenny marking mine, and being a complete star and fantastic friend, she scribbled a load of answers in for me so that I wouldn't get too bad a score. Now that's what I call a mate! I was marking Rosie's paper and she'd done nearly as badly as me by the looks of things, so I tried to put a few answers in there, too. Rosie was obviously thinking about the swimathon as well, judging by all the empty spaces on her answer sheet!

Unfortunately, our little bout of "helping" was spotted by beady-eyed Emma Hughes, one of our sworn enemies, the M&Ms. BAAAD news...

"Mrs Weaver, Kenny and Lyndsey are cheating!" she said at once, sticking her hand in the air.

Kenny scowled at her and I gave her a dirty look. Interfering cow! Just because she was a mega-brain maths-head!

Mrs Weaver hates people telling tales, but she's also pretty hot against cheats, too. "Kenny and Lyndsey, bring your answer sheets here," she said crisply. "I think I'll mark the rest of those, thank you very much."

Emma gave us this whopping great smirk, like she'd just won a prize. In fact, if there was a prize going for smugness, she would have won the gold medal.

Mrs Weaver soon cut her down to size, though. "And Emma, we don't like tell-tales in this class, so you can wipe that grin off your face," she said. "Now then! Let's see if we can get through the rest of this test without any more dramas!"

Kenny and I exchanged looks. Trust one of the M&Ms to stick a big fat nose into our business.

As you probably guessed, me and Rosie didn't do very well on the maths test in the end, thanks to old supergrass Hughesy. Mrs Weaver handed our papers back, not looking very impressed.

"Tomorrow's Friday, and it'll be the last test of the week, as you all know," she said, "so let's see if we can get some better scores, please! I don't know what's up with you all this morning but some people obviously aren't at their brightest. Let's do some long division, to see if THAT will get your brains in gear."

Ugh! She was in a bad mood now, if she was making us do MORE maths. We were all relieved when it was break time, and we could get outside for a breather. But by now, Rosie was grumpy and fed up, I was feeling completely thick as I'd got all the long-division sums wrong, and even Kenny was still a bit growly after being told off.

Luckily, Fliss managed to cheer us up. "I've been thinking," she started, as we went out into the playground.

"Does it hurt?" Kenny muttered.

Fliss ignored her. "Shall we have the sleepover at mine tomorrow night?" she said. "We could make it a swimming theme, you know, because of the swimathon!"

"Will your mum mind us coming round?" I asked. Everything's been a bit hectic at their house lately, what with the twins coming along. Even Fliss hasn't looked her usual immaculate self – which tells you how much hard work they must be!

Fliss shrugged. "No, I'm sure she won't mind," she said. "She suggested it, anyway. Said she didn't want to let appearances slip, just because of the twins."

"What a trooper!" Frankie said. "That's what we like – a mum who knows the importance of a good sleepover." Then she frowned. "What do you mean by a swimming theme though?"

Fliss's face fell. "Well... actually, I couldn't think of anything specific," she confessed.

"I was hoping one of you lot would have some ideas."

"We could... er... all wear blue, like water," Rosie suggested, screwing her face up as she said it. "No, that's far too boring!"

"Practise swimming up and down the bath?" I said.

"We could watch *Titanic*!" Fliss said, brightening. She must have seen that film about fifty times by now. "Although I suppose that's more about drowning than swimming, isn't it?"

"It's a shame it's not summer – we could have had a water fight in the back garden," Kenny said wistfully.

Frankie looked up at the grey cloudy sky, and shivered. "Not on your nelly!" she said firmly. "We'd all get hypothermia!"

"Well, everyone get their thinking heads on, anyway," Fliss said. "We've got a whole day to come up with other stuff we can do – so everyone bring something with a swimming theme to my house tomorrow night, six o'clock sharp!"

CHAPTER THREE

Most Fridays, without fail, my first thought when I wake up is, "Yay! Sleepover day!" My mum reckons it's the only day of the week when she doesn't have to physically drag me out of bed! I always wake up feeling really excited and raring to go. OK, so there's a day of school to get through before we can start having fun, but somehow, that goes much faster when you know there's a lovely sleepover waiting for you at the end of it. And then after THAT, it's the weekend!

I was halfway through my breakfast when

I suddenly remembered the swimming theme Fliss had suggested.

"Mum, have you got any ideas about what I can take to Fliss's tonight?" I asked, and then told her the whole story. My mum used to be a teacher and now runs a playgroup, so she always has lots of good ideas.

She thought for a minute as she buttered her toast. "Does it have to be strictly swimming, or could it stretch to playing in water, do you reckon?" she said. "Because we've got beach balls and rubber rings and things you could take along."

"I've got *Jaws* on video if you want to borrow it," said Tom, my second oldest brother. "As long as you PROMISE not to wreck it."

"And as long as no-one's going to have nightmares," Mum put in at once.

"Hmm, maybe," I said slowly. Even though I love all animals, sharks are a bit scary, I think – but I certainly wasn't going to tell Tom that!

"There are lots of silly swimming hats in the dressing-up box, too," Mum said. "You know, the ones Auntie Vera gave us, with all the plastic flowers on them?"

"Yeah, excellent!" I said, with a giggle. "I can just see Kenny in one of them!"

"Come on," she said, standing up and taking her toast with her. "Let's see what we can find!"

The others must all have been thinking hard about what to bring for the sleepover, too, because on Friday night, when we got to Fliss's, there was a whole heap of weird and wonderful goodies.

Kenny had brought flippers, face masks and a blow-up lilo.

Frankie had a rubber ring, two pairs of arm bands and some goggles.

Fliss had her *Titanic* video (surprise, surprise!) and had dug out a selection of swimming costumes for Rosie to choose from.

And Rosie had brought along her Supa Scuba board game, plus a huge bag of mini Mars bars. "I thought we'd get hungry with all this talk of swimming," she explained.

"Right," said Fliss uncertainly. "So what are we going to do with this lot, then?"

We looked at the wacky assortment in front of us, and all five of us burst out laughing at the sight. Good point – what WERE we going to do with it all? Kenny put on a bright pink swimming hat with plastic daisies that I'd brought along and batted her eyelashes, and we all laughed even harder.

"Suits YOU!" we all chorused, still giggling.

Frankie was getting a familiar kind of gleam in her eye, though. The kind of gleam that said, "Idea alert!".

"Uh-oh – Frankie's brain is ticking away," I said. "Any second now she's going to say..."

"I've got an idea!" she said, grinning. "How about a dressing-up obstacle race?"

"A what?" Rosie spluttered.

"We'll race against the clock, one by one," Frankie told us. "You start off over here, by the door, yeah? Then you have to jump into the rubber ring, pull it up over your head and off again, then put on the flippers and run over to the window..."

"Then put on a swimming hat and goggles and catch the beach ball three times," Kenny said, getting into the idea.

"Then stuff a mini Mars bar in your mouth and say, 'Swimathon, swimathon, swimathon!' while doing a forwards roll on the bed!" I said. The game was getting crazier by the second!

"Then pretend to snog Leonardo diCaprio," suggested Fliss – of course! – giving the video box a passionate kiss.

"Then put on both pairs of arm bands, lie on the lilo and 'swim' your way back over to the door," Rosie said. "And the fastest time wins!"

By now, we all felt giggly again. "I bet no-one ever thought of a swimming game like THIS before," Frankie said proudly. "Who wants to go first?"

"Me!" we all said at once.

It was the funniest game we'd played in absolutely *ages*. It was funny to do it, but even funnier to watch as, one by one, we all made ourselves look completely mad with the full swimming gear over our jeans and T-shirts. The sight of someone trying to do a forward roll in flippers, with a Mars bar hanging out of their mouths, saying,

"Swimathon, swimathon, swimathon!" was just *soooo* hilarious! At one point I seriously thought I was going to wet myself laughing.

HIC!

Oh no, I'd got the hiccups instead!

"Hicathon, hicathon, hicathon!" gurgled Kenny, clutching her stomach.

"Thanks for the... HIC! sympathy!" I said, elbowing her in the ribs. "Oh no, quick, someone help me!"

My hiccups are legendary in the Sleepover Club. I'm the only one who seems to get them, and I often get them at really TERRIBLE times, like if we're spying on someone, or trying to think about something serious. The others have come up with about a million different ways to cure me but I'm quite hard to stop, once I get going.

This time, it was Rosie's turn to have a brilliant idea. She picked up one of Kenny's face masks and slapped it on my head, pushing the snorkel into my mouth. "There," she said proudly. "Now just breathe through the snorkel. That'll sort you out!"

I thought Frankie was going to explode

with laughter at the sight of me, red-faced, trying to breathe through this rubber tube.

"I wish I had my camera," she moaned, rolling on the bed. "You don't half look a sight, Lyndz!"

I had to turn away from the others to stop myself getting even gigglier, and concentrated on breathing slowly through the snorkel. And do you know what? It actually worked!

I took the face mask off after a minute or so, and tried breathing normally. Yes, it really had worked. "Rosie, you're a genius!" I said gratefully. "I'll just have to carry an emergency face mask around with me for the rest of my life now!"

"Right, who hasn't had a turn yet?" Frankie said, checking her piece of paper with our times written on. "Fliss! Starting position, please!"

"Remember, don't waste too much precious time snogging Leonardo," Kenny warned. "Every second counts!"

"Oh, he's worth it," Fliss assured her, smacking her lips together eagerly.

Rosie consulted her watch. "Ready, steady, go!" she called.

Once all five of us had had a go – and then ANOTHER go because it was so much fun – we all lay on Fliss's big pink double bed, sucking strawberry laces and getting our breath back.

"Fastest time was... Kenny!" Frankie said, checking her sheet.

The rest of us groaned. Typical! Kenny always won every race we ever did.

"Wait," said Frankie, cupping her ear, "do I hear disapproval from the crowd?"

Me, Fliss and Rosie booed loudly. "Fix!" Rosie shouted.

Frankie pretended to consult her sheet again. "I'm afraid the judges have decided not to award first prize to Miss Laura McKenzie after all, as that's far too boring and predictable," she said solemnly. "So the next fastest time is... Rosie, Lyndz, Fliss and Frankie!"

"YEAH!" we all cheered.

"Cheats!" yelled Kenny, throwing a Smartie at Frankie, who caught it neatly in her mouth.

"And I'm just hearing that Miss Laura McKenzie has been banned from all future competitions for violent and aggressive behaviour," Frankie started – until Kenny jumped on top of her and started bashing her with a pillow. "Aaargh!" Frankie squealed.

I don't know why, but ALL our games seem to end in a pillow or teddy fight. Of course, that was our cue to launch in with a full-scale attack. Before long, everything was flying wildly around Fliss's room, and all five of us were breathless with giggles. Rosie was bashing people with the rubber ring, Frankie was walloping Kenny with a flipper, and the air was black with flying mini Mars bars.

But unfortunately, there was suddenly a loud SMASH! We stopped what we were doing at once, getting that awful sinking feeling as we looked around, wondering what we'd broken this time.

We all saw it at the same moment.

"The vase!" exclaimed Fliss in horror, running over to check the damage.

Uh-oh. Why is it ALWAYS the most expensive thing in the room that gets broken? Fliss has lots of nice stuff in her bedroom, but of course, it just happened to be this cut-glass vase that had been knocked over and smashed by a flying flipper.

"It's ruined," Fliss said shakily, looking like she was about to burst into tears. "Mum's going to kill me!"

"Are you sure it can't be glued together again?" I said, going over to have a look. "You never know, it might look all right with..." But my voice trailed off as I saw just how broken it was. Not even the most careful, patient person in the world would have been able to fix it. It was game over for the vase, big-time.

And of course, who should knock at the door and walk in just then, but Fliss's mum with a tray of lemonade and biscuits. We all looked at the floor guiltily, and Fliss shuffled in front of the bits of glass quick as anything. Maybe we could get away with it, if Fliss's mum didn't notice...

But Fliss's mum DID notice how quiet it had gone in the room, and how no-one was meeting her eye, and how her own daughter looked as if she was about to cry any second.

"What's going on?" she asked at once, her voice sounding sharp. "Felicity?"

"Er... nothing," Fliss said weakly, forcing a smile.

Fliss's mum plonked the tray of drinks down and marched straight over. When she saw all the broken glass, she gave this big angry sigh. "Oh, Felicity! Not my vase!"

Then she looked around and took in all the mess and swimming stuff that had been thrown everywhere. "What on earth has been going on in here?" she asked, sounding really mad now. "You've only been up here half an hour and look at the state of this bedroom! Felicity, you're more trouble than the twins!"

"We were practising for the swimathon," Fliss said lamely.

"Oh, were you now?" her mum said, her lips getting tighter and crosser by the second. "Well you can think again about entering this swimathon now, young lady – the only money you're going to be raising is money to buy me a new vase!"

"But Mum..." Fliss started, looking horrified at the thought.

"But nothing!" she snapped. "Now all of you come away from this broken glass while I clean it up. Go on, run along. You can set the table for dinner, and make yourselves useful for a change. SHOO!"

CHAPTER FOUR

No-one felt like giggling or laughing now. We crept out of the room before Mrs Proudlove could get any madder, all feeling sick with guilt. No offence to Fliss, but that is the WORST thing about having sleepovers at her house – her mum gets all uptight about us spilling drinks on the carpet or breaking things or being too noisy. And as you just saw, Mrs P can be one scary lady if you get on the wrong side of her, which we often seem to do.

But this time, it had gone really wrong. Now it looked as if Fliss wasn't going to be able to take part in the swimathon – and that was mega-bad news. In fact, it was an utter catastrophe!

Even worse, as we were going downstairs, we heard two loud wails start up from the twins. All the shouting had woken them up – and Fliss's mum would be even crosser now!

"I can't believe it!" Fliss exploded, once we were in the kitchen. "I can't believe she'd be so mean that she won't let me take part!"

She looked dead upset about it, her bottom lip all trembly.

I put my arm around her. "I bet she'll come round once she's calmed down," I said sympathetically. "I bet you anything! How much do those vases cost anyway? Maybe we could all chip in and get one to say sorry."

Fliss sighed heavily, getting a heap of knives and forks out of the drawer with a clatter. "Oh, about a hundred pounds, I should think," she said. "Seriously! It was cut-glass! That's expensive, isn't it?"

"Maybe we could get her a bunch of flowers tomorrow?" Frankie suggested.

"My mum's a sucker for them – it's the best way I've found to get back into her good books."

Fliss shook her head. "Mum gets hay fever," she said. "Flowers make her sneeze her head off – and that'll put her in an even worse mood!"

"Chocolates?" Rosie said. "Everyone loves chocolates, don't they?"

Fliss shook her head again. "Not at the moment," she sighed. "Mum's eating really healthily because she's breastfeeding. Chocolate is off the menu in this house!"

We laid the table in silence. No-one could think of any other ideas.

"Oh, but you *have* to do the swimathon!" I burst out in the end. "It's not fair, you getting punished for something any one of us could have broken!"

"If YOU don't get to take part, then I won't, either," Rosie said suddenly. "It's only fair!"

"Hang on, hang on!" Kenny said hastily. "There's no need for that! I'm sure Fliss wouldn't want anyone else to miss out, would you, Fliss?"

We all held our breath as Fliss turned the idea over in her head.

"After all, it's not very nice for all those poor disabled children who would lose out if we didn't make any money for Whizz-Kidz," Kenny said craftily, before Fliss could speak. It was obvious that Kenny *desperately* wanted to take part!

"That's true," Fliss said. "No, you'll all have to do it without me. I can... I can cheer you on from the side," she added bravely. "And count your lengths and things like that."

"That would be good," I said encouragingly. "It wouldn't be the same without you there at all, Fliss."

"Oh!" She clapped a hand to her mouth suddenly, looking desolate. "But that means I get to miss the party if I'm not taking part! And I was planning to wear my new party dress and everything! Oh, NO!"

"I'm sure you can still come," Frankie said. "We can pretend you're my sister or something."

"Mmmm," said Fliss, but she still looked downcast. "Oh, I hope Mum changes her mind!"

"Oh, so do I!" I said. "We all do, Fliss!"

* * *

Dinner was a bit of a quiet affair that evening. We're never normally THAT rowdy at Fliss's because her mum is a real stickler for manners, but this evening we were all on our absolute best behaviour, even Kenny. No-one dropped anything, no-one spoke with their mouth full, no-one put their elbows on the table. If the dinner ladies from school could have seen us, they would have been gobsmacked!

Andy, Fliss's step-dad, glanced round at our mournful faces and laughed. "Blimey, what's happened?" he said. "Did someone murder Westlife while I wasn't looking?"

Fliss scowled, and said nothing.

"Don't pull faces, Felicity," her mum said at once. "You'll get wrinkles."

Well, it didn't look like Fliss's mum was in a better mood yet, anyway. I glanced at her quickly without her noticing, and she looked really tired and fed up.

There was silence, except for the *clink clink scrape* of our knives and forks.

Andy tried again. "No, seriously," he said. "What's happened? It's not like you five to be so quiet! Is it a sponsored silence or something?"

"They've managed to break one of my favourite vases, that's why they're so quiet," Fliss's mum said.

"Fliss got in trouble, Fliss got in trouble!" Fliss's brother Callum sang out in delight.

Fliss scowled furiously at him – forgetting the wrinkles advice – but said nothing.

"Oh, I'll have a look at it later, I'm sure it's mendable," said Andy.

"Thanks, Andy!" Fliss said gratefully. She's lucky to have such an ace step-dad. He's dead easy-going, which balances Fliss's mum out a bit. Also, he's a bit of a real-life Handy Andy, too, and is always working on some fantastic DIY project around the house. And unlike my dad, he actually manages to finish them, too!

"I don't think it IS mendable actually," Fliss's mum sniffed.

"I'm going to save up for a new one, Mum," Fliss said meekly. She had a face like a hot tomato, as Frankie would say. "I'm really, really sorry!"

Fliss's mum softened a bit at that. "No, you don't have to get a new one," she said. "I know it was an accident, so let's just leave it at that." Then she forced a bright smile. "Now then! Who wants some more quiche?"

"Yes, please," Kenny and me both said at the same time.

"Does that mean I can still do the swimathon?" Fliss asked hopefully.

"We'll see," her mum said.

Andy winked at Fliss while Mrs Proudlove was cutting slices of quiche, and Fliss gave him a wobbly smile in return. She still wasn't taking anything for granted!

Oh dear, I hope I'm not making Fliss's mum sound like a real witch in all this. Most of the time she's dead nice, honestly. But I think she's just been run off her feet with two tiny babies. And I suppose different people care about different things, don't they? I mean, if someone had damaged something I really loved, like Alfie or Buster, I'd be hopping mad as well. And if someone had messed up one of my mum's playgroup projects, she'd have been cross about it, too.

The rest of the sleepover was a bit on the subdued side, even though it looked as if we'd just about been forgiven for the vase thing. We played Rosie's board game a couple of times and finished off the sweets, and you'll be pleased to hear that everything else in Fliss's room stayed safely unsmashed.

"Well, with a bit of luck, you might be OK to do the swimathon after all, Fliss," I said, when we'd all got into our sleeping bags that night. "Fingers crossed, anyway."

"Eyes crossed, toes crossed, legs crossed," Fliss said fervently.

"Arms crossed," Frankie said, after a moment.

"Er... ears crossed," Rosie said with a giggle.

"How can you cross your ears?" Fliss said at once. "You'd have to have really massive ones!"

"You'd have to be an elephant!" I said.

"Or Emma Hughes!" Frankie chuckled.

"Bum-cheeks crossed," Kenny said, with a snigger.

"Oh, Kenny!" Fliss said indignantly. "That's gross!"

"Fancy being able to cross your bum-cheeks!" Rosie said. "You'd have to have a really massive—"

"Yes, I think we get the message!" Fliss said quickly. She gets a bit prim if we start getting too rude!

"Shall we go for our first training session tomorrow, then?" Frankie said, changing the subject. "I brought my kit with me."

"So did I," I said.

"Me too," Kenny said. "Coo-ell! It's a date!"

And with that lovely thought in our heads, we all fell asleep.

It wasn't until I woke up the next morning that I realised I was meant to be having a riding lesson that day. D'oh! It's not like me to forget something as important as that!

"I'm really sorry, you guys," I said at breakfast, "but I'm riding today – so I won't be able to go swimming after all. But you might as well go without me. I'll just try and squeeze in a swim after school this week instead."

"Oh, actually, I can't go either," Rosie said quickly. "I... er... I promised Mum I'd help her with the shopping."

"So you'd rather go to Tesco than swimming?" Kenny said scornfully, heaping peanut butter on her toast. "Hmmm... Rosie Cartwright – freak or unique?"

"Total freak," Frankie said, but with a grin at Rosie to say she didn't mean it.

But Rosie flushed, and looked embarrassed. "No, of course I wouldn't rather go to Tesco," she said. "But I've promised, haven't I? I can't just phone up and say I've changed my mind, I'd rather go out with my friends!"

"Parents!" Frankie sighed. "They're always getting in the way of fun."

"Well, if there's only going to be three of us, maybe we should wait until tomorrow and ALL go then," Fliss suggested. "We've got to do this properly, haven't we? We don't want to make fools of ourselves by being unfit on the big day!"

"Unfit for what?" Fliss's mum said, coming into the kitchen just then. "Morning, girls!"

"Morning, Mrs Proudlove!" we chorused

politely. Even though we'd heard the twins crying a couple of times in the night and knew she must have been up feeding them, she looked like she'd just stepped off the pages of a catalogue, with not a hair out of place – before she'd even had a cup of coffee! The day my mum strolls down for breakfast looking like that is the day I've woken up in the wrong life, I'm telling you.

"Oh, we were just talking, nothing much," Fliss said uncomfortably.

"We were talking about the swimathon," Kenny said, flashing her biggest smile at Mrs Proudlove. "We were saying how hard we're going to have to practise for it, how we're all going to have to get really fit."

"I shouldn't think you'd have a problem there, Kenny," Fliss's mum said, smiling back.

And then I sussed what Kenny was up to. Very sneaky! We all know Fliss's mum is well into her keep-fit classes, and is always urging Fliss to have tennis lessons, swimming lessons, ballet lessons and all that... So if we could make her think that the swimathon was going to be something super-healthy for her daughter to do, then she might give Fliss the go-ahead! Never mind the fact that what Fliss was most interested in was dolling herself up for the party afterwards. Her mum didn't have to know about that bit.

"Well, I'm planning to do one hundred lengths, so even I'm going to have to train like mad," Kenny said, still trying to hammer home the point.

"And I'm going for half a mile," Frankie said.

"Really? That IS impressive!" Fliss's mum said. "Gosh! I didn't know you were all such good swimmers!" You could see the cogs whirring in her brain as she thought about it some more. And then she said casually, "So, how many lengths do you think *you'll* do, Felicity?"

Fliss's eyes went wide in surprise. "You mean... you mean I can do it? I can do the swimathon?" she said, jumping up from the table.

Mrs Proudlove laughed. "Yes, you can," she said. "I think it sounds like an excellent idea – as long as you use up all your energy in that swimming pool, NOT in my house!"

We all laughed, and grinned at Fliss, who had run over to hug her mum. "I'll be the most careful daughter you've ever had!" she promised. "And I'm going to swim further than I've ever done before – you just watch me!"

CHAPTER FIVE

Re-SULT! We were all dead chuffed for Fliss. Like I'd said, it just wouldn't have been the same without her there. We're definitely at our best when all five of us are on board – and now we would be!

Fliss couldn't stop grinning. I think she was massively relieved to have made things up with her mum, too. The two of them normally get on so well together. Fliss always gets upset if they fall out, or if she gets told off for something.

I glanced at my watch and gulped down the rest of my tea when I saw the time.

"Oops! Dad's gonna be here any minute to pick me up," I said. "I'll just go and clean my teeth!"

Rosie got up, too. "Can I cadge a lift?" she asked. Her house is on the way to the riding stables.

"'Course you can," I said, charging upstairs. "But we'd better hurry!"

Lucky for me, my dad's always about ten minutes late. Sometimes it really bugs me but today I didn't mind at all! Me and Rosie had just got all our stuff together when...

BEEP! BEEP!

"That'll be him," I said, rolling my eyes at the loud horn outside. "I don't think my dad knows how to knock on the door – sorry, Mrs Proudlove!"

The others waved us off at the front gate. "So eleven o'clock sharp tomorrow at the swimming baths!" Kenny yelled as we got in the car. "Catch ya later, alligators!"

"In a while, crocodiles!" Rosie and I both bellowed back, waving madly.

Rosie was a bit quiet in the car. Then she said, "Lyndz, can I tell you something? A secret?"

"'Course!" I said, in surprise, wondering what was coming. But just at that moment, my dad started telling us how Buster had got stuck in the cat flap the night before.

"All you could see was this brown and white bottom wiggling around frantically," he chortled loudly. "And Truffle got really cross because she wanted to go out, so she swiped his bottom with her paw – and that got Buster even more wound up, and he gave this great howl!"

We all laughed at the thought. Then I turned back to Rosie. "What is it?" I said in a low voice.

She shook her head. "Oh... nothing. It doesn't matter," she said. "I'll tell you later."

I wanted to press her on the subject as she was looking all troubled, but my dad was still chuckling away in the front as he told us how they finally got Buster free, so it wasn't really a good time for secrets. I squeezed her hand instead. "OK, tell me later," I said.

I couldn't help wondering what was bugging Rosie as I got changed at the stables for my riding lesson. She seemed really bothered about something – and she had been ever since Kenny had first mentioned the swimathon. Was it something to do with that, maybe? Or perhaps there was some problem at home? Hmmm!

However, I'm sorry to say, I must be a very bad friend indeed, because as soon as I saw Alfie, the thought of Rosie went right out of my head again. All I could think about was how utterly beautiful he was, and how much I wished I had my very own horse.

In fact, I must be a really TERRIBLE friend, because I managed to forget all about Rosie until the next day, when I saw her outside the swimming baths. One look at her pale face, and it all came back to me. What on earth was up with her?

Kenny was there too, tapping impatiently on her watch. "Come on, come on! Where are the others?" she said. "Oh look, here comes Fliss in Andy's car. About time!"

"And there's Frankie on her bike," I said, spotting a familiar red mountain bike coming up the road. "All present and correct!"

"And ten minutes late," grumbled Kenny. "Come on, you two! Look lively!"

Inside the baths, Kenny seemed to know absolutely everyone there.

"Hello, love," said a smiley old lady on the front desk. "How are you today?"

"Fine thanks, Vi," Kenny grinned. "Five junior swims, please. Oh, and can we have some sponsor sheets for the swimathon, too?"

"Yes, certainly!" Vi said, pulling out a sheaf of forms from under the desk. "One for each of you, is it? There we are. Good luck!"

Then as we went through the ticket check, two athletic-looking men in tracksuits smiled at Kenny.

"Here comes trouble!" said one of them.

"All right, Freckles?" said the other.

"Hi, Rob, hi, Mike," Kenny said, handing our tickets in.

Fliss looked disappointed. "I was hoping the dark-haired one would be that Nige you were telling me about," she whispered when we were out of earshot.

"Nige?" Kenny spluttered. "Oh, no. Nige is *much* better looking than those two. You're in for a treat, girl!"

Fliss looked delighted. "Ooh, really?" she

said breathlessly. "Quick, let's get in the pool and check him out!"

Once we were in the changing rooms and Kenny had called out hellos to two other girls, we started getting our swimming gear on. Kenny and Frankie were well prepared and had their costumes on underneath their clothes, so after about ten seconds, they were bundling their bags and coats in lockers and rushing off.

"See you in there!" Frankie shouted.

It always takes me ages to get changed. My mum says she despairs of me on school mornings, when it seems to take me half an hour to get dressed. But Rosie and Fliss are both pretty slow, too, luckily!

Fliss was all excited about clapping eyes on this Nige bloke, and started adjusting her new cozzie. It was pretty cool – slim and silvery, with a wicked little logo on the front.

"What do you think?" she asked, giving us a twirl.

"It makes you look like a fish, Fliss," said Rosie.

Fliss looked miffed. "That's not very nice!"

she pouted.

"I'm sure Rosie meant it nicely," I said hastily. "You meant a dolphin or something, didn't you, Rosie Posie?"

Then Fliss started picking fretfully at the nail polish on her toes. "Oh, no, it's all chipped!" she said in horror. "This is a total catastrophe!"

Rosie and exchanged looks and tried not to laugh. "Fliss, no-one's going to be looking at your toes, don't worry about it," I said.

"They might!" Fliss retorted anxiously. "Oh, look at the state of it! Honestly!"

"Ooh dear," Rosie teased. "Yes, I can see it from here. What a mess! Whatever are you going to do now?"

There was no reply, as Fliss had moved on to fretting about her hair. Fliss has really lovely hair. It's long, thick, shiny and golden, and it's her absolute pride and joy. She was stuffing it into a red swimming cap for all she was worth, anxiously peering at her reflection in the mirror to see if there were any loose strands poking out.

"I don't want any of those nasty chemicals

ruining my hair!" she said defensively, catching the pair of us staring at her open-mouthed. "Gervase says it's in very good condition right now, so I don't want any chlorine to touch it!"

"Yes, Gervase said that to me last time I went in for a trim," Rosie said, teasing again. We all know Rosie's big sister Tiffany cuts the whole family's hair! "He told me, darling, whatever you do, just don't let that nasty chlorine ruin your gorgeous brown locks!"

I got the giggles as Rosie tossed back her short, mousy hair dramatically and batted her eyelashes.

Fliss pouted. "You may scoff," she said, "but don't come crying to me when you go bald before your eleventh birthday!" And with that, she stalked off to the lockers, her nose in the air.

"Oh, Fliss, we were only teasing!" I called out, trying to stop giggling. Bald! As if!

I pulled my costume on hurriedly as she went off. "Blimey, Fliss being ready before us two – makes a change, doesn't it?" I said.

"Are you nearly done?"

"Er... nearly," Rosie said, peeling off her T-shirt about as slowly as humanly possible. "You go on ahead, Lyndz."

"Nah, don't be daft, I might as well wait," I said, piling everything into my bag and sitting down on the bench. "Hey, do you want to borrow some goggles? I bought two pairs in case someone had forgotten to bring any."

"Thanks," she said, as I passed them over. She pulled up Fliss's costume and put her arms through the straps.

"Right!" I said, jumping up. "Let's do it!"

But Rosie was still sitting in the same spot. "Er, Lyndz..." she began, sounding nervous.

"Yeah?" I asked, fishing out two 10ps for the lockers.

"Lyndz... I haven't been swimming for a while," Rosie said.

I shrugged. "Neither have I," I confessed. "But I suppose it's one of those things like riding a bike, isn't it? You never forget how to do it. I bet you'll be bombing up and down with Kenny in no time!"

She shook her head and looked at the floor.

"Actually, I think I HAVE forgotten how to do it," she said cautiously. Then it all came out in a rush. "Actually – I can't swim at all!"

I stared at her in shock. "Can't swim?" I echoed. "What, never? You've never swum in the sea on your holidays, or anything? 'Cos that counts, you know!"

Rosie looked really miserable by now. "We can't all afford summer holidays, you know!" she almost shouted, still not looking at me.

There was this awful silence. I didn't know what to say. I told you Rosie was prickly, didn't I? Right now, she looked as if she was wishing she hadn't said anything at all. Then she started pulling her swimming costume off again.

"I've got a bit of a cold anyway, I probably shouldn't get my hair wet," she said quickly.

"Oh, Rosie," I said, still not sure how to handle this. I didn't want to get my head bitten off again. "Why don't you just come in the shallow end with me? You can keep your feet on the bottom all the time, and no-one has to know!"

There was a silence again, while Rosie

thought about it. I rushed on, trying to persuade her. "I'm a rubbish swimmer, anyway," I said. "We can just mess about together and have a laugh. And anyway, doggy paddle is dead easy, I can show you how to do it, if you want?"

Rosie heaved this huge sigh but still said nothing.

"Come on," I said encouragingly. "I won't say a word to the others if you don't want me to."

She looked up then. "Promise?" she asked.

"On Buster's life," I said solemnly. "You never know – you might even enjoy yourself!"

CHAPTER SIX

So THAT was what Rosie had been worrying about all this time. No wonder she'd been trying to make excuses to get out of the swimathon! Still, at least she'd told me now. Better out than in, as my mum always says.

We went into the main pool, to see Kenny tanking up and down with this fantastically splashy butterfly. Fliss was doing a graceful back stroke, her arms poker straight whenever she lifted them, and Frankie was doing a speedy crawl. Rosie was all quiet as I slipped into the shallow end.

"Brrr!" I shivered. "It's freezing!" Then I caught sight of Rosie's face looking even more uncertain. "Well, you soon warm up!" I said quickly. "Look – and it's not even deep, I've got both feet on the bottom here!"

Rosie smiled self-consciously and lowered herself in.

"Let's just pretend we're warming up," I said. "Here – grab hold of the side, and let your bum float up to the top."

"What, take my feet off the floor?" she asked, looking nervous.

"Yeah – watch me," I said, showing her. "You just float, all right? And then if you kick your legs behind you, you can stay up. Like this, see?"

Rosie watched me, but didn't try it herself.

"Then if you ever get worried or scared," I continued, "all you have to do is put your feet on the bottom again and stand up! Bob's your uncle!"

"Right, OK," Rosie said at once. I could tell she hadn't liked me saying the word "scared". Rosie prides herself on being a bit of a tough cookie. "So if I hold on to the side, and let my feet float up..."

"That's it!" I said encouragingly, still kicking away with my legs. "Now kick your legs up and down!"

She did it for about ten seconds and then hastily stood up again. "I did it! Did you see that?" she asked. She looked really pleased with herself.

"Nice one!" I said. "Try again!"

Slowly but surely, she got the hang of it. Soon we were both chatting away about school things as we held on to the side and kicked.

Just then, Kenny splashed up beside us. "What's this, a mothers' meeting?" she demanded. "Are you two going to stay there yapping all day?"

Rosie bit her lip anxiously and looked at me.

"Just warming up!" I said casually. "I'd have thought you'd know that, Miss Gold Medal winner!"

"All right, all right!" Kenny said. "See you in a bit." And she zoomed off again, strong legs kicking out behind her.

We carried on with our own leg kicks. "Hey, Rosie," I said, "you're halfway to swimming now you can do this, you know! This is all your legs have to do for doggy paddle, and then you scoop the water in front of you with your hands, like a dog does. Watch!" And I did a width of doggy paddle and back again to show her.

She was still clinging on to the side when I got back. "Don't rush me," she said. "I'm just going to stick at this for a while, if it's all the same to you!"

"All right," I said. "I will, too, then. Now what were you saying about Emily Berryman?"

Fliss was the next one to splash up beside us. She was all red-faced. "Six lengths without stopping!" she said triumphantly. "I'm just going to get my breath back now."

"Nice one!" I said. "We've decided to start our training by just working on our legs, eh, Rosie?"

"Yeah, that's right," Rosie said.

"That's a good idea," Fliss said distractedly, looking around. Then she turned back to us, cupping her hand to her mouth. "You'll never guess what I've just done!" she said in a low voice.

"Weed yourself," Rosie suggested wickedly.

"Ugh! No!" Fliss protested. "Rosie!"

"What have you just done?" I prompted, before Fliss went all grossed out and stroppy.

"I've only just gone and made a fool of myself in front of the most gorgeous boy in the pool!" she wailed.

"What, Nige?" I asked with interest.

"No, Kenny says he isn't working today, worse luck," Fliss said. "No – him, that boy on the diving board at the moment!"

"Why, what did you do?" Rosie asked. "Don't tell me – he spotted your nail varnish was chipped."

"No – I crashed right into him!" Fliss said with a giggle. "We were both doing back stroke and somehow our arms got all tangled up together! It was *sooo* embarrassing!" She ducked her head suddenly and went pink. "Oh no, he's looking at me! Oh no!"

"Oh NO!" me and Rosie chorused, laughing.

"Couldn't you just DIE?" I said dramatically.

Fliss stuck her nose in the air. "Oh, you two wouldn't understand!" she said haughtily, and swam off again.

We started kicking our legs back and talking again. Then Rosie stood up, looking serious. "OK, show me doggy paddle again," she said. "I think I've got the hang of the legs thing now."

"OK," I said, lifting my arms out of the water so she could see them. "You make a sort of scrabbling movement like this, yeah? Just think of Buster swimming in Cuddington Lake! And then while you're doing your arms like this, you just kick your legs behind you like we've been doing."

"And that's it?" Rosie asked.

"That's it," I said. "Watch!"

I swam a few metres away and turned around to face her. "See if you can do it to here," I said. "It's only a couple of strokes!"

Rosie didn't look convinced. "What, so I just let my feet go up, and do that with my hands?" she asked.

"Yeah, launch yourself forward a bit, and kick!" I said. "Go on, give it a try!"

Rosie looked dead nervous, but did as I said, and launched herself forward. Her head went right underwater, and she stood up choking and gasping. "Oh! I think I swallowed half the pool!" she said, looking frightened.

"What on earth are you two doing?" Frankie said, swimming up to us. "I haven't seen either of you do a length yet!"

"Oh, neither of us have been swimming for ages, so we're just taking it easy," I said quickly. I was getting very good at covering up Rosie's secret! "Anyway, why do you look so fed up?" I asked, changing the subject.

"Oh, nothing really," she said, glancing over her shoulder to check no-one could hear her. "Well, all right, then. Kenny's gone off with two of her mates from swimming club and they're having races. And she didn't even ask me if I wanted to join in!"

Blimey, it was all kicking off at the pool today!

"Actually, I think I'm going to get out now anyway," Frankie said. "I'm getting a bit cold – and I've done eighteen lengths so I'm dead tired."

"Eighteen! That's brilliant!" I said, feeling a bit guilty at only having done a couple of widths. "Shall we get out now, too?" I asked Rosie.

"Yeah!" she said eagerly. "I feel quite tired after all our training!"

We got showered and changed and waited for the others in the café upstairs. I don't know about you, but swimming always makes me feel hungry, and I wolfed down a plate of chips in no time.

Rosie was still a bit quiet, and it wasn't until Fliss and Kenny had joined us that she spoke. "I've got something to say," she started, in the same serious voice I'd heard earlier. "And it's really hard to tell you, but..."

"What?" asked Kenny through a mouthful of cheeseburger.

"Go on," I encouraged. I had a feeling I knew what was coming...

"I'm really sorry, everyone, but I definitely WON'T be doing the swimathon," she said. "No, let me finish!" she said, as a chorus of moans went up around the table. "I... I lied to you before. I won't be able to do twenty lengths for the swimathon – because... because I can't swim!"

There was a silence, just like back in the changing rooms when she first broke the news to me.

"There, I've said it!" she said, her face all tight. "So you can all have a good laugh at me, all right?"

"No-one's laughing," I said comfortingly.

"You should have said before," Kenny said.

"Can't SWIM?" Fliss was incredulous. "How do you get to be your age and not be able to SWIM? My brother can swim and he's only SEVEN!"

"Fliss!" Frankie said crossly. "Don't be a jerk!"

"But I thought I saw you swimming with Lyndz?" Kenny said. She still looked as if she couldn't believe it. As a person who could do anything, it was always a bit of a shock to her when one of us failed to match up.

Rosie shook her head. "Lyndz was trying to teach me, but..." She sniffed, and then gave this great sob. Then a tear rolled down her cheek. Rosie the tough cookie – crying?

It was almost unheard of!

I passed her my serviette, which only had a teeny bit of ketchup on it. We all looked at each other as she blew her nose.

"Rosie," said Kenny, "wouldn't it be worth learning how to swim if it meant you could raise some money for Whizz-Kidz?"

"Yeah, it's such a good cause," Frankie said. "You said so yourself!"

Rosie shook her head. "I won't be able to learn to swim in two weeks!" she said in a small voice. "I'll never be good enough!"

"You could always do it separately," I suggested. "You could ask people to sponsor you for LEARNING to swim. OK, it might take a bit longer, but at the end of it, they'll all have to cough up!"

"Yeah, maybe when you get your ten-metre badge or something," Kenny said. "Good idea, Lyndz!"

"You ARE a water sign after all," mystic Fliss chimed in. "You're probably a natural, you know!"

Rosie looked at me and spluttered out a laugh. "I don't know if Lyndz would agree with that," she said.

"You were really good considering you'd never done it before," I said earnestly. "Honestly! You were dead brave! And your leg kicking was brilliant!"

Rosie sighed and wiped her eyes. "It's about time I learned to swim, really," she said, as much to herself as to anyone else. "Maybe I'll ask Mum if I can have a few lessons."

"That's the spirit!" Frankie cheered. "You go, girl!"

CHAPTER SEVEN

I don't know about you, but I reckon Rosie was dead brave, owning up like that. She's normally such a proud person, it must have practically killed her. You've got to give her respect for that, haven't you?

The funny thing was, she cheered up straight afterwards, as if she felt really relieved to have it off her chest. It must have been horrible for her, trying to keep it to herself all this time when the rest of us could talk about nothing else.

I gave her a big cuddle when we were saying goodbye. "Feel better now?" I asked.

"Yeah," she said, starting to look more like her usual cheerful self. "Thanks, Lyndz. You're a real mate and a half!"

I went a bit pink. "Let me know what your mum says about lessons!" I said, getting on my bike. "See you all at school tomorrow!"

I got back home just in time for our Sunday roast – and I was still starving, even after the plate of chips I'd munched through. Afterwards, I felt all sleepy from the combination of exercise and lovely food. So I decided that before I went out to collect sponsors for the swimathon, I'd cuddle up on the sofa and watch *EastEnders* with my snuggle blanket, and maybe even have a little nap...

Do you have a snuggle blanket? I know it's a bit babyish of me to still have one, but I can't get to sleep without it. I've had it since I was born and it's this little pink fleecy cot blanket that Mum used to cover me up with. These days, it's more of a grey-ish colour than pink, and there are a few shiny bits where the fleece has worn away, but it's still one of my favourite things in the world.

Anyway, the only thing was, I went up to fetch it from my bedroom – and it wasn't there! I looked everywhere – under the pillow, under the duvet, even down the side of the bed in case it had got wedged down there but... no snuggle. Weird! I just couldn't think where else it could have got to. Mum hadn't put it in the wash and all my brothers swore they hadn't touched it – so where was it? The thought of having to spend the night without it was just... unthinkable!

"Well, it WAS getting a bit ancient, wasn't it?" Mum said. She was trying to be comforting but I could feel my bottom lip getting all trembly at the thought of never having my snuggle to sleep with ever again.

"Mum, you haven't thrown it out, have you?" I asked in horror, preparing myself for a dash to the dustbins.

"No, of course not!" she said, stroking my hair.

"Where can it be, then?" I moaned for the twentieth time.

"Tell you what," she said quickly as my bottom lip went all trembly again, "while you're out getting sponsors from the neighbours, I'll have a good look for it in the washing basket and in your bedroom. It can't have vanished into thin air, can it?"

"No," I sighed. "I suppose not."

"So can I be the first one to sponsor you for the swimathon?" she said.

I smiled at her. My mum is the best person in the world at cheering me up. "Yes, please!" I said, handing over the form.

"How many lengths do you think you'll do then?" she asked, fishing out a pen from her handbag.

"Only about ten," I said sheepishly. "Not like Kenny – she's going to do a hundred, she reckons!"

"Ten lengths is brilliant," Mum said firmly. "I don't know if I could swim ten lengths these days. Does 50p a length sound all right to you?"

50p a length? That was... that was five POUNDS if I could manage ten lengths! "Awesome!" I said, feeling much happier now. "Thanks, Mum!"

By the time I came back from collecting

sponsors up and down our street, I was feeling even better. So far, if I managed to swim ten lengths at the swimathon, I was going to raise thirty pounds for Whizz-Kidz! Wasn't that brilliant? Then my dad chipped in the same amount as my mum, and even Tom and Stuart sponsored me at a flat two pounds each, whatever I managed to do. So that made nearly FORTY pounds – after just one afternoon of trying! I was so chuffed, it made me absolutely determined to swim ten lengths at the swimathon – if not more!

The only bad thing was that despite turning my room upside-down, Mum still hadn't found my snuggle. It was a real mystery.

If I thought my missing snuggle was bad, the next day, something else went missing that was even more upsetting. Truffle! Normally, when I get home from school, she's sitting waiting on the front wall for me to make a fuss of her. The only thing that ever stops her from sitting there is if it's pelting down with rain or freezing cold. But even then, she'll sit in the front window, watching out over the street. She's always there, anyway, that's what I'm trying to say. And as I come up the road, it's the first thing I'm looking out for – my lovely fat stripy tabby, who rolls around excitedly whenever she sees me.

But on this particular Monday, she wasn't on the wall, even though it was quite warm outside. She wasn't even on the windowsill inside the house. In fact, I couldn't see her anywhere.

Now, if you've got a cat, then you'll know they're a bit unpredictable and tend to do just what they want. The thing about Truffle though, is she's *utterly* predictable ("Nice but dim", my dad calls her) and she rarely does anything out of her little routine. It was really strange, her not being there. I couldn't even think of another time she hadn't met me from school.

"Truffle!" I called softly, just in case she was hiding behind the wall. Nothing – not even a whisker.

Maybe she's playing with the other cats, I thought to myself, or maybe she's busy trying to catch a mouse or something.

Maybe she's all curled up nice and warm inside and is too sleepy to wait for me today.

But even when I got in the house and searched around, and called her name out a hundred times, there was still no sign of her. I was so upset and worried, I burst into tears on the spot.

"What if she's trapped in a cupboard somewhere and can't get out?" I sobbed, this awful picture going into my head of poor old Truffle mewing frantically and scrabbling to get out. "What if... what if she got into someone's CAR and they've driven off? That happened in a story I once read!"

Dad made me a cup of tea and put some extra sugar in it – "For shock," he said. Then he pulled me over to sit on his knee. "Truffle hates cars, doesn't she?" he reminded me. "She's scared of them – she won't go near a car, let alone get INTO it."

"But what if... what if someone's catnapped her?" I wailed. That had happened in another book I'd read – where someone was stealing pedigree cats and selling them to make money.

Dad gave a snort. "Who would want to steal that great fat thing?" he said, passing me his handkerchief. "Sweetheart, cats like exploring – think how nosey Truffle is! She's probably having a whale of a time hunting around someone's garage or in someone's back garden. She'll be back in time for tea, I bet you!"

I stopped crying then. Food! Now that was a thought. There was no way Truffle would ever miss a meal. She was the first one at the food bowls every night, meowing excitedly and rubbing around Mum's legs as if she hadn't eaten for a week. "You're probably right," I said, blowing my nose. "I hope so, anyway!"

The phone rang just at that moment. "That'll be her now," Dad joked. "Saying, 'Don't let those other greedy cats have my share of the Whiskas'!"

I giggled as I went to get the phone. It wasn't Truffle, of course, but it WAS Rosie, sounding dead excited and breathless.

"Lyndz, guess what? I've just asked Mum about swimming lessons – and she thinks it's a brilliant idea!" she whooped. "She said yes!"

"Excellent!" I said, feeling pleased for my mate.

"And she phoned the swimming baths and there's a beginners' class called Ducklings every Wednesday night after school – so I'm starting this Wednesday!" she said, gabbling the words out in her excitement. "I can't wait! I can't believe I'm going to learn to SWIM after all this time!"

"Good for you," I said. "The others will be dead chuffed, too – especially mystic Flisstic, with all her talk of water signs!"

"And Lyndz, I..." She suddenly slowed down. "I just want to say thanks for being so nice the other day, you know..."

"What are friends for?" I said warmly. "Any time!"

But even Rosie's words couldn't make me happy as it got to tea time and there was still no sign of Truffle. That was when I REALLY started to get worried. Truffle miss a meal? It was absolutely unheard of.

"It's not as if she's going to starve," Stuart said unsympathetically when I searched around his bedroom for her. "Think of all the winter blubber she's put on lately – she could go without food for a week, I reckon."

"That's not the point!" I said. "She LOVES her food – she wouldn't miss her dinner for anything! Something really awful must have happened if she's not here. Something like..." A terrible thought hit me at that moment. "What if she's been run over?" I gasped, bursting into tears all over again. "What if she was hit by a car?"

Once I'd had that horrible thought, I just couldn't get it out of my head. I dragged Tom out to help me look up and down our street for her, convinced I was going to find her bleeding and battered in the gutter somewhere. But there was STILL no sign of her.

"Well, at least we know she hasn't been run over now," Mum said comfortingly when we came back again. "Now, Lyndz, it's way past your bath time. Come on, a nice hot bubble bath will make you feel better. Doctor's orders!"

It was one of the worst evenings of my life. I cried all the way through my bath and then went to bed and cried myself to sleep. Something mega serious must have happened for Truffle not to be around, and I just couldn't bear it if I never saw her again. Where was she and why hadn't she come home?

CHAPTER EIGHT

Well, something serious HAD happened all right – and luckily we found out the very next morning. It wasn't a moment too soon, I can tell you. I'd barely slept a wink worrying about Truffle. Every time I felt myself dropping off, I swore I could hear a faint mewing, and then I'd sit bolt upright in bed again, wondering if I'd dreamt it or if I really had heard her.

I must have got some sleep though, because the next thing I remember is my mum bursting into my room, a great big smile upon her face. "Lyndz! Lyndsey! Wake up!" she was saying. "We've found Truffle! Dad's just found her!"

PING! I was completely awake in a micro-second and jumped out of bed. "Where? Oh, where is she?" I cried, feeling this great burst of happiness inside me. "Is she OK?"

Mum smiled. "She's fine – in fact, she's more than fine," she said, and started leading me to the stepladder that went up to the loft.

"She's up THERE?" I gasped. My dad's been converting our loft into a play room but it's been strictly out of bounds to us for weeks. Wouldn't you know it, it was the ONE place I hadn't looked.

Mum nodded and we started going up the steps. "Yes – and she's got company!" she said. "Dad went up there first thing to see if he'd left his spirit level in there – and he had a bit of a surprise!"

Company? What was Mum talking about? I shuddered suddenly – I hoped she didn't meant that Truffle had found a rat's nest or something!

But once we were up in the loft, I realised exactly what she meant. Kittens! Four gorgeous little tabby and black kittens cuddled up with Truffle, who was looking well pleased with herself!

"Oh!" I said in delight. "Truffle's a mummy!"

"So that's why she's been looking even fatter lately," Mum laughed. "And that's not all – look what she's made her little nest out of!"

I peered closer – and sure enough, I recognised the grey-pink blanket they were all lying on. "My snuggle!" I said. "Oh, Truffle, I don't mind YOU taking my snuggle!"

"She must have thought it looked like a good bed for them," Mum said. "Mind you, I don't know if it'll ever be the same again..." she added doubtfully.

"Oh, I don't mind," I said happily, stroking Truffle who was rumbling away with proud purrs. "She can have it!"

Well, I really had to DRAG myself out of the house that morning, I can tell you. Those four kittens were just the sweetest things you've ever seen! One was all tabby with white paws, just like its mum, one was all black with a little white tip to its tail, and the other two were a mixture of black, white and tabby stripes. Cuter than cute! Now, I just had to think of some good names for them!

I made Truffle a special breakfast of tuna fish (her favourite) and brought it up to her with a saucer of milk. I reckoned she deserved it after having four little babies in one night.

"Do you think she'd let me pick one of them up?" I asked Mum hopefully.

Mum frowned. "Not just yet," she said. "Give it a few days. Mummy cats are very protective of their kittens, even though I'm sure she knows you wouldn't hurt them. Just give them a few gentle strokes for now, OK?"

I held my breath and gave the tiny Truffle lookalike a little stroke on its head. The kittens all had their eyes shut still and were making sucking noises with their tiny pink mouths. "Aren't they just *soooo* cute?" I whispered, giving Truffle some big strokes to show her that I still loved her the best.

"Yes, and isn't Mrs Weaver going to be just *soooo* mad at you when you're late for school?" Mum reminded me. "Come on –

chop, chop! I'll put some toast in for you while you're getting dressed."

"Oh, do I absolutely have to go to school today?" I begged, even though I knew the answer.

"Yes, you absolutely do!" Mum said. "Come on – the sooner you get there, the sooner you can come home and see them again! I don't think they'll be going anywhere just yet!"

I knew she was right, but it didn't make it any easier for me to leave the house that day. Then a great thought struck me as I was putting my coat on. "Mum, do you think we could have a KITTEN sleepover on Friday?" I said. "Oh, can we?"

"Yes, I should think so," she said, smiling at my excited face. "As long as you're very careful. If Truffle thinks for a second that the kittens are in danger, she'll get very upset. She might abandon them – or she might even kill them. Understand?"

I nodded solemnly. There was no WAY I would let that happen! Then I skipped all the way to school, feeling as if a huge weight had lifted off me after the miserable night I'd just had. Instead of having three cats, we now had SEVEN!

The rest of the week was great. There's nothing like some cute wobbly-legged kittens to put a smile on your face, believe me. Every day after school, I rushed straight home to see them, and spent hours up there, stroking Truffle and watching the four babies staggering around feebly. Their eyes opened after a couple of days and were a bright blue.

"Can we keep them, Mum?" I begged every night. "Please? Can we keep just one of them?"

"I don't think so, love," she'd say gently. "I'm going to put a note up in the Post Office window when they're six weeks old and we'll find some good homes for them to go to."

"But they want to stay with their mummy!" I'd plead. "Oh, go on, Mum!"

If my dad was in earshot, he'd put his foot down at once. "We've got enough animals in this house already!" he said firmly. "Any more and we'll have a full-scale zoo on our hands!"

I wasn't the only one who was feeling happy. Rosie had her first swimming lesson and took to it straight away. "I can't believe it's so much FUN!" she said. "All these years and I've been too scared to try – and now I think I'm going to love it!"

Kenny and Frankie were well into their swimming, too. They both went training in the week and were really gearing up for the swimathon.

And Fliss was over the moon because she thought baby Joe had smiled at her when she was helping her mum bath them one night – even though Frankie put the dampeners on by saying that it was probably just wind!

It's funny how just a few things can turn your mood around, isn't it? There I was at the beginning of the month, thinking all sorts of gloomy things about February, and here we were, all five of us having a fantastic month. Babies, kittens, swimming... life was pretty good!

On Friday night, I was bursting with pride when the other four came back to mine for the kitten sleepover. Anyone would have thought they were *my* kittens, not Truffle's! I was all set to go straight up to the loft and show them before anything else, but Mum had other ideas.

"If you five clomp up there in your great big school shoes, you'll frighten them," she said firmly. "Anyway, I've just made some strawberry shortbread, so how about if you take your shoes off, sit down for five minutes and THEN go and see them?"

"All right, all right," I grumbled, but I didn't really mind. My mum's strawberry shortbread is wicked!

The best thing about the sleepover was that Mum had said we could name the kittens. With four kittens and five of us, there weren't quite enough for us to choose one name each, so we were going to have to think about them very carefully.

"Fluffy," said Fliss, stroking the little tabby.

Kenny pulled a face. "Pickles," she suggested for the black one. "That was the name of the dog who found the World Cup when it had been nicked."

"You can't call a kitten after a DOG!" Rosie said indignantly. "How about Tigger for this one? He's got a lovely stripy tail."

"Tigger is cute," I agreed. "What about Barney?"

"Nah – Barney Gumble from *The Simpsons*!" Kenny said at once, and did a big Barney-type burp.

"Or Barney Rubble," Frankie pointed out. "What about... Rover?"

"NO!" we all said – a bit too loudly actually, as it made two of the kittens jump.

"I've got it!" Kenny said. "Filbert!"

"Oh, that's quite sweet," Fliss agreed. "Filbert, I like that!"

"Well, I don't," I said, shaking my head at Kenny. "And you won't either, Fliss, when you realise that Filbert Street is Leicester City's football ground! Nice try, Kenz!"

"No dogs, no football," Rosie said, wagging her finger like Mrs Weaver does.

"OK, OK, if you insist!" Kenny grumbled. "So how about... Zebedee?"

We all liked Zebedee. At last! Something we agreed on! But at that point, Mum came up and told us we should leave the kittens in peace for a while, so we went to my bedroom to decide on the others.

Fliss had the brainwave of calling them Eeny, Meeny, Miny and Mo, which got shouted down at once. And Frankie wanted to call them after characters from *The Hobbit*, her favourite book. We said no to that, but agreed that Bilbo was a nice name.

"One of them looks like he's wearing a little black bib after all," Fliss said.

"Bilbo, not BIBLO!" Frankie said, swatting her on the head. "Derrrr!"

So we had Tigger for the black and tabby one with a stripy tail, Biblo – I mean Bilbo – for the black and tabby one with a black bib, Zebedee for the one who was pure black, and...

"I think Lyndz should decide on the tabby one's name," said Rosie. "After all, they ARE her kittens."

"OK," I said at once. "She's the only girl of the four – so I vote we call her Millie."

"Oh, that's so sweet!" Fliss said at once. She loves girly names.

"That's Millie, not MIB-lie, Fliss," Kenny pointed out.

Fliss promptly chucked a gobstopper at Kenny – which bounced right off her head!

The kitten sleepover was great fun. We played Cat's Got The Measles until we were all out of breath, and then after tea, when it was getting dark, Rosie suggested playing Sardines around the house. "Well, cats love fish, don't they?" she pointed out. Fair enough!

We had one last peek at Tigger, Bilbo, Zebedee and Millie, and then it was time for bed.

"Everyone ready for a swim tomorrow?" Kenny yawned once we were all in our sleeping bags.

"YAY!" we all cheered, Rosie's voice louder than anyone's.

And with that, I fell asleep straight away and dreamed about fluffy, purring kittens all night.

CHAPTER NINE

One thing you CAN'T say about the Sleepover Club is that we're boring. There always seems to be SOMETHING funny happening to us!

I mean, take a simple thing like a training session in the swimming baths. You'd think that would be quite straightforward, wouldn't you? Get in the pool, do a few lengths up and down, shower and change, go home again. Oh, no. Not if you're called Lyndz, Fliss, Rosie, Frankie and Kenny, anyway.

It started off fine. We all got changed – no hanging back in the changing rooms this time for Rosie! – and were in the pool in no time. Kenny, Frankie, Fliss and I all decided to do some lengths, while Rosie asked one of the lifeguards for a float to practise doing some widths with.

No sooner had she spoken to him than Fliss was at her side, eyes nearly popping out of her head. I swam up too, to see what was going on.

"He is GORGEOUS!" Fliss breathed, clutching Rosie's shoulder in excitement. "That lifeguard! He must be Nige, mustn't he? Kenny said I'd like him – and she was right!"

I stared at the blond lifeguard as he chucked a float in Rosie's direction. "There you go!" he called, smiling at her.

Fliss gasped. "Did you see that? He smiled at me! Oh, he is just..."

"Fliss, I think he was smiling at Rosie," I said, catching Rosie's eye and trying not to smirk.

"No, it was definitely me," Fliss said, her eyes fixed on the lifeguard as he walked back to his seat by the side of the pool. "No doubt about it! Right, well, I'm going to HAVE to get to know him better. Any ideas?"

"Pretend to drown?" Rosie said, giggling. "Then he'll have to dive in and rescue you!"

I knew Rosie was only joking, but Fliss – of course – took it as deadly serious.

"Brilliant idea!" she said, her eyes lighting up. "Rosie Cartwright – you are a genius!"

Rosie and I looked at each other, shaking our heads, as Fliss splashed off towards the deep end.

"What is she like?" I groaned. "I just know this is going to go pear-shaped!"

Rosie and I carried on swimming as normal. Kenny was teaching me breaststroke, which I was getting the hang of, but after a few lengths, I started to get a stitch, so I decided to have a breather at the deep end. Which was quite good timing, as it happened, because it meant I was just in time to see...

"Help! Somebody help me!"

You guessed it – Fliss, doing her best feeble filly impression, splashing around frantically. Honestly, I just couldn't believe she was going along with Rosie's silly idea!

Sometimes I wonder about Fliss – she doesn't half do some daft things.

"Help! I've got cramp!"

SPLASH!

All I saw was a blur of white as one of the lifeguards did this fantastically flashy dive into the pool. As he surfaced and began a strong crawl over to Fliss, I bit my lip and couldn't help letting out a chuckle. It wasn't the blond bombshell who'd dived in – it was a different lifeguard all together!

And if THAT wasn't funny enough, the look on Fliss's face as she realised who was swimming towards her was such a classic, I nearly swallowed half the pool laughing! For the lifeguard who'd swum up to help her was practically bald and looked about the same age as my dad. *Baywatch*, he was not!

"Oh, oh, I think it's all right now," I heard Fliss say. "Thanks, but…"

"Let's just get you out and have a look at you anyway," Baldy said, towing her firmly to the side and scooping her out of the pool. "Now, cramp did you say? That's nasty. Which leg was it?"

"Er, er... this one," Fliss said distractedly, pointing at her left leg. She was looking around the pool, trying to find the other lifeguard – the one that didn't look like someone's dad with great big warts all over his face. "Er... where's Nige?"

The lifeguard was rubbing her calf vigorously, and looked up in surprise when she said that. "Nige? That's me, love!" he said proudly. "Nigel Jackson – pool supervisor! You're lucky I was there to spot you!"

"Er, yes, thanks," said Fliss miserably, as she realised she'd been set up by naughty Kenny. "I really think it's better now, thank you."

"Sure you don't want the kiss of life while I'm at it?" he leered, giving her a wink.

"No!" she said, turning bright red. "No, honestly, I'm fine now – I'll get back in the pool. Thank you."

"Well, any time you want your life saving, just give me a shout!" he said as she slid hurriedly back into the water. "All part of the job, you know!"

Frankie and Kenny had joined me at the side of the pool to watch Nige's mercy mission. The three of us were helpless with laughter when Fliss swam up to us. Red-faced and practically spitting with rage, she was NOT in a good mood any more!

"I see you've met Nerdy Nige!" Kenny hooted, with a wicked grin. "Sexy, isn't he? I told you you'd like him – and it looks like he quite fancies YOU, too!"

"I could kill you for that, Kenny!" Fliss grumbled. "I'm never going to trust anything you say EVER again!"

"You've got to admit, it WAS funny though," I gurgled. "Your face, Fliss!"

Fliss pursed her lips up crossly, but before she could reply, Kenny pointed to the shallow end of the pool.

"Talking of faces..." she said, "look who's just about to get in the pool!"

"Oh, who?" Frankie said, squinting into the distance. "I can't see that far without my specs!"

Fliss and I followed Kenny's pointing finger – to see the M&Ms sitting at the shallow end.

"The M&Ms!" I told Frankie with a shudder. Then a thought struck me. "Hey, I hope they're not going to have a go at Rosie for not being able to swim," I said fiercely. "They're bound to say something mean to her."

That's what the M&Ms – Emma Hughes and Emily Berryman – are all about, if you didn't know. Mean, spiteful, cruel. No wonder they always hang around together – no-one else can stand them!

"Oh, Rosie can look after herself," Kenny said confidently. "But I think I'll just find out what they're up to, swimming on a Saturday morning like this. They're usually sitting on their fat bums watching TV at home!"

"I wonder if they're going to do the swimathon as well?" Frankie said, raising her eyebrows as Kenny swam off.

"Oh, I BET they are!" I said gloomily. "Which means they'll be at the party afterwards and everything!"

"Talking of the swimathon," Fliss reminded us, "haven't we got some training to do?"

Oops! We really weren't getting much swimming done this morning! So off we set again, trying to build up our stamina with more lengths. My legs have always been quite strong from horse-riding, but doing doggy paddle has always made my arms feel really tired really quickly! I thought they must be a bit weak and wimpy, but for some reason, I was finding breaststroke a lot easier, arms-wise. Maybe my plan to do ten lengths wasn't so optimistic after all!

Kenny passed me just then. "Hey, Lyndz, that looks really good!" she said, stopping and treading water beside me.

"Thanks!" I said, grabbing hold of the side. "I think I'm getting the hang of it now. Might even try it in the swimathon!"

Kenny nodded. "You should – it's much less tiring than doggy paddle," she told me. Then she nodded her head over to where the M&Ms were. "By the way, they ARE going in for the swimathon as well, can you believe? Who would have thought the M&Ms would do anything to help anyone?"

"Weird!" I agreed. Very out of character!

Kenny and I both swam off in different directions. Just as I reached the shallow end again, I heard this great squawk from the other end of the pool. It sounded like Kenny, so I looked over to see what was happening. It WAS Kenny – being attacked by both Ms! I couldn't quite see what was going on, but she told me later that they'd both gone for her underwater and tried to yank her swimming cozzie off her! I told you they were evil, didn't I?

Lucky for Kenny, she's not only a great swimmer but she's really strong as well. After a bit of a struggle, which involved her biting Emily's hand, she managed to get them both off her and did a surface dive deep underwater where they couldn't catch her. Then she skimmed along the bottom of the pool like a torpedo, coming up for air about ten metres away from them! She did a ferocious crawl down to the shallow end where I was.

"They're going to regret that!" she said furiously. "Fancy thinking they could get the better of me!"

Rosie floated up next to us, and soon Frankie and Fliss joined us, too. "What's the plan of action, Kenz?" Rosie said, knowing that Kenny would HAVE to have revenge.

There was no way on earth she was going to creep out of the pool without giving the M&Ms a taste of their own medicine!

"I think a dive-bombing campaign might wipe the smirks off their faces," Kenny said through gritted teeth. "Does everyone know how to do that?"

"Bombs?" Fliss gaped, looking terrified. "What do you mean, bombs?"

"I'm not going to blow up the pool, don't worry!" Kenny laughed. "Dive-bombing is where you dive AT someone – only instead of stretching your body out, you hug your knees in to your chest really tightly so that you land with a real splash. If you do it properly, you can completely drench someone. And if all five of us do it at the same time..."

Rosie was looking worried. "I'm not sure..." she said uncertainly. "I don't really want to go in the deep end yet."

"Don't worry, Rosie, four of us will still make a good splash," Kenny said with a grin. "Much as I'd love you to join us, encouraging a non-swimmer to throw herself in the deep end goes against all the safety rules I had to learn for my gold medal!"

Rosie laughed and looked relieved. I was, too. Kenny has this mad reckless streak in her, and even though I know she's still got enough sense not to put one of us in REAL danger, she does sometimes get a bit carried away – especially where a revenge plan is concerned!

"How can we do this without looking really obvious?" I said practically. After all, the M&Ms weren't totally stupid. They would have no illusions that Kenny was about to try and pull one over on them.

Sure enough, the M&Ms were keeping a close eye on us from a safe distance. "They know we're up to something," Fliss said. "How can we catch them off guard?"

"They're in the middle of the pool so they can't get out very quickly," Frankie pointed out. "So…"

"So, we'll have to act quickly," Kenny said, taking charge. "I've got it. We all get out of the pool as if we're going to go home. That'll throw them off the scent. Then, just when they think they've got away with it, we all run up the side as quickly as we can. Hopefully they won't have time to get very far – and then it's dive-bombs away!"

"Excellent!" I said, grinning from ear to ear. It's always good to sock it to the M&Ms!

However, you know the saying about best-laid plans? Well... that's kind of what happened to us. We got out of the pool and started walking towards the exit. Then...

"Now!" said Kenny, and the four of us turned tail and charged up the side of the pool.

"Bombs away!" yelled Kenny when we drew level with the startled M&Ms – and we all threw ourselves off the side, tucking our knees up as Kenny has told us.

SPLASH! SPLASH! SPLASH! SPLASH!

It was a direct hit! The M&Ms were surrounded and completely splattered!

But before we could even celebrate, we heard...

PEEEEEEP!

A whistle blew shrilly, and the next thing we knew, Nerdy Nige was standing over us.

"All of you – out now! Cannonball diving is against the pool rules! You should know better, Laura! Come on – OUT!"

CHAPTER TEN

So we all ended up getting chucked out of the pool, which wasn't QUITE what Kenny'd had in mind. But we all agreed it had been well worth it to see the looks of terror on Emma and Emily's faces as we came hurtling towards them. Excellent!

Still, it meant we had cut our training short again – and with the swimathon only a week away now, it really was time to knuckle down to some SERIOUS training – no more mucking about! So on Tuesday night AND Thursday night, me, Kenny, Frankie and Fliss went along to the baths to practise, while

Rosie went to her Ducklings class on the Wednesday night.

I felt a bit better, having some extra practice sessions under my belt, but I was still a bag of nerves the next Saturday morning. I just HOPED I could manage my ten lengths – I still hadn't been able to in our training sessions.

The swimathon was turning out to be a much bigger event than we'd first thought. The spectators' gallery was totally packed, and we searched the crowds for familiar faces.

"There's my mum and Spike!" I squeaked, spotting Mum waving madly at us.

"And there's Andy!" Fliss said excitedly. Mrs Proudlove was staying at home with the babies, but Andy and Callum had come along to cheer Fliss on.

"There's my mum and dad – and there's Rosie!" Kenny said, giving them a wave.

I felt a pang when I saw Rosie's face, and wished she was taking part with us. I think she'd felt a bit left out, being the only one of us spectating, but I'd promised I'd go and sit with her once I'd finished. Let's face it, I was hardly going to be in the pool for very long!

Then someone blew a whistle and everyone got in the pool. Luckily the four of us had all been put in the morning session, so at least we were starting at the same time – even if we were split up straight away. Kenny went in the fast lane, Frankie and Fliss went for the medium lane and I plumped for the slow lane. I had to hand in my form to one of the many lap-counters at the side of the pool, and then another whistle went which meant it was time to start!

We all had numbers pinned to our swimming hats which made it easy for the lap-counters to keep track of how we were getting on. I was number 54, which felt lucky to me – after all, there were FIVE in the Sleepover Club and FOUR kittens. How could I go wrong?

One... two... three... four... The first four lengths were pretty easy, after the three training sessions we'd put in that week, and especially now I'd sussed out breaststroke. I kept thinking about what Kenny had said to me – "Slow and steady. Don't burn yourself out in the first ten minutes – PACE yourself!"

Five, six... Slow and steady, I kept telling myself. Slow and steady. The rules were that you weren't allowed to stop for more than ten seconds at the end of each length. When I'd done six lengths, I allowed myself a quick breather.

"You're doing great!" my lap counter told me with a big smile, and then off I went again. Slow and steady, slow and steady....

Seven, eight... My arms were starting to feel like heavy weights now and I was puffing away like a steam train. Could I really do another two lengths when I was feeling so out of breath?

And then, over the roar of the crowd, I heard...

"Go on, Lyndz!"

It was Rosie! Even though I was feeling absolutely whacked, I knew I had to give it my best shot. The "slow and steady" chant in my head changed to "Forty pounds! Forty pounds!" If I kept reminding myself how much money I was going to raise, I HAD to be able to do another two lengths!

Nine. Nearly there! I heaved a huge sigh and pushed off from the side again. Just one more length to go and I would have swum 250 metres, which was more than I'd ever done in my life! The shallow end was getting nearer and nearer – I was really going to make it! Just a few more strokes and... TEN! I'd done it!

"That's ten lengths!" my lap-counter smiled – as if I didn't know!

And then, I don't know how it happened, but I was feeling so proud of myself and there was so much adrenaline rushing around inside me – that I turned round again and started doing another length!

ELEVEN! I hung on to the bar at the end of that one and felt completely drained. That was it – no more energy now. I was totally WALLOPED! I dragged myself out of the pool, legs like jelly. But even though my body was tired and my heart was still pounding away and I had no breath left, I felt like I'd just broken a world record. Eleven lengths!

I looked up at my mum, who was holding both thumbs up at me and grinning, and I felt dizzy with happiness. I put my towel round my shoulders to keep warm and walked down to the shallow end where my lap-counter – Julie – signed my form. "Well done!" she said warmly. "Are you pleased?"

I nodded, too out of breath to speak, and went to have a nice hot shower. I'd done it! I really had DONE it!

The others had done pretty well, too – in fact we'd all hit our targets. Fliss had done 22 lengths, Frankie had done 32 and Kenny had finished on a whopping 110 lengths. Not a bad showing for the Sleepover Club, eh?! All together, Frankie worked out that we had raised nearly two hundred pounds between us. Talk about a result!

By the time the party started that evening, we were all really up for a top night. We had some seriously good swimming to celebrate, after all! It felt a bit strange going to the swimming baths all dressed up in our best clothes – and inside, it was even stranger. A stereo system and dancefloor had been put in at the side of the pool, there was music blaring out and fairy lights everywhere, and the pool itself was lit by the underwater lamps, so it looked dead festive.

Nerdy Nige grabbed a microphone. "Could I have your attention, please, ladies and gentlemen?" he said, and everyone went quiet. "Now, I'm not going to make a speech..." he began.

"Hooray!" cheered Kenny, and a few people laughed.

Nige forced a smile and tried to ignore the interruption. "I'm not going to make a speech, but I AM going to say a very big thank you to everyone who took part today," he said hurriedly, before Kenny could say anything else. "You've all done a brilliant job – so make sure you enjoy yourselves tonight. This one's on us!"

The music started up again, and a couple of people went on to the dancefloor.

"Well, well, look who it isn't," Kenny said with interest, pointing to the M&Ms, who were sitting at the edge of the shallow end, their feet dangling in the water. "You know, I still think we owe them one, don't you? After all, it was THEIR fault that we all got chucked out last week..."

"What are you thinking, Kenny?" Rosie asked curiously.

"I'm thinking... THIS!" she said – and without another word, she charged over, intending to push them both into the pool.

But the M&Ms must have heard her running up behind them. They dodged out of the way just in time – and Kenny ended up over-balancing and flying into the pool herself, fully-dressed, with a loud squeal!

The M&Ms collapsed with laughter – and so did we, as everyone turned to stare at crazy Kenny. Kenny promptly started showing off, doing handstands underwater, and walking on her hands.

Almost breathless with laughter, Frankie turned to the rest of us, her eyes bright. She took off her specs and carefully put them on one of the food tables. "What do you reckon? Shall we join her?" she asked with a big grin.

"What – jump in?" Rosie asked, looking a bit nervous.

"It's only the shallow end," I reminded her.

"How about if we all hold hands and do it? That way you'll be quite safe."

"I don't know..." Rosie said uncertainly.

"Come on!" said Fliss. "You can go in the middle, how about that?"

Then Rosie grinned. "OK – as long as you don't let me drown!" she said.

"Trust us!" Frankie assured her, grabbing one of her hands.

So me, Frankie, Rosie and Fliss ended up running up to the edge holding hands and then all throwing ourselves into the water, screaming and laughing our heads off.

And so that was how the Sleepover Club went...

Well, that's about the end of the story, really. There's just time to tell you two bits of good news. First of all, Rosie got her ten-metre swimming badge last week and was well chuffed about it. She says she's DEFINITELY up for taking part in the next swimathon. She's even decided what she wants for her next birthday – a swimming costume!

Now that's good news – but here's some even better news. After begging, pleading and two weeks of being the best-behaved daughter in the world, Mum and Dad have said we can keep one of the kittens. We did a family vote on which one we'd keep and Zebedee was everyone's favourite. He's sitting here with me right now – can you hear him purring?

Prrr, prrr, prrr, he's saying – which means, this is Lyndsey Marianne Collins and Zebedee the kitten saying goodbye for now. See ya!

Whizz-Kidz

THE MOVEMENT FOR NON-MOBILE CHILDREN

Help get disabled children whizzing!

We all enjoy running around, playing with friends, going shopping or playing sport. With your help, disabled children can enjoy these things too.

Whizz-Kidz provides specialised wheelchairs and walking frames to help disabled children whizz around independently.

Why not do something to raise money at your school and help us to get more disabled children moving? How about a sponsored swim or even a non-uniform day?

For more fantastic fundraising ideas, or to tell us what you would like to do to raise money at your school, call our Schools Fundraiser (or get your teacher to call) on 020 7233 6600 or write to us at **Whizz-Kidz**, 1 Warwick Row, London SW1E 5ER.

You can also check out the **Whizz-Kidz** website at www.whizz-kidz.org.uk.

Whizz-Kidz needs YOUR help!

Reg Charity No. 802872

39

Sleepover Girls Go Karting

It's thrills and spills for the Sleepover Club when they pack up their kit for a weekend of karting. But can they beat the awful Josh, track champion and son of the owner? Or will the mates lose the challenge and end up – shock, horror! – as Josh's cheerleaders?

Get out of the pit lane and speed on over!

40

Sleepover Girls Go Wild!

The Sleepover Club is off to the local wildlife park, Animal World, for the day! Will Frankie enter the Spider House? Will Fliss go anywhere near the snakes? But then Kenny starts teasing Lyndz about what Hissing Horace the python's having for supper. Little does she know what she's started...

Pack up your sleepover kit and let's PIG OUT!

Order Form

To order direct from the publishers, just make a list of the titles you want and fill in the form below:

Name ....

Address ....

....

....

Send to: Dept 6, HarperCollins Publishers Ltd, Westerhill Road, Bishopbriggs, Glasgow G64 2QT.

Please enclose a cheque or postal order to the value of the cover price, plus:

UK & BFPO: Add £1.00 for the first book, and 25p per copy for each additional book ordered.

Overseas and Eire: Add £2.95 service charge. Books will be sent by surface mail but quotes for airmail despatch will be given on request.

A 24-hour telephone ordering service is available to holders of Visa, MasterCard, Amex or Switch cards on 0141- 772 2281.

Collins
An *Imprint* of HarperCollins*Publishers*